**T**his is George.

He lived with his friend, the man with the yellow hat.

He was a good little monkey and always very curious.

This morning George was curious the moment he woke

up because he knew it was a special day...

At breakfast George's friend said, "Today we are going to celebrate because just three years ago this day I brought you home with me from the jungle. So tonight I'll take you to the animal show. But first I have a surprise for you."

# *Curious George*
## Rides a Bike

## H. A. REY

WALKER BOOKS
AND SUBSIDIARIES
LONDON • BOSTON • SYDNEY • AUCKLAND

First published in Great Britain 2004
by Walker Books Ltd, 87 Vauxhall Walk, London SE11 5HJ

2 4 6 8 10 9 7 5 3

Published by arrangement with Houghton Mifflin Company

This book has been typeset in Gill Sans MT Schoolbook

Printed in China

British Library Cataloguing in Publication Data:
a catalogue record for this book is available from the British Library

ISBN 1-84428-507-3

www.walkerbooks.co.uk

He took George out to the yard where a big box was
standing. George was very curious.

Out of the box came a bicycle. George was delighted;
that's what he had always wanted. He knew how to ride
a bicycle but he had never had one of his own.

"I must go now," said the man, "but I'll be back in time

for the show. Be careful with your new bike and keep

close to the house while I am gone!"

George could ride very well. He could even do
all sorts of tricks (monkeys are good at that).

For instance he could ride this way,
with both hands off the handlebars,

and he could ride this way,

like a cowboy on a wild bronco,

and he could also ride backwards.

But after a while George got tired of doing tricks and

went out into the street. The newsboy was just passing by
with his bag full of papers. "It's a fine bike you have there,"
he said to George. "How would you like to help me
deliver the papers?"

He handed George the bag and told
him to do one side of the street
first and then turn back
and do the other side.
George was very proud
as he rode off with his bag.

He started to

deliver the papers

on one side of the street

as he had been told.

When he came to the last house

he saw a little river in the distance.

George was curious: he wanted to know

what the river was like, so instead of

turning back to deliver the rest of the papers

he just went on.

There was a lot to see at
the river: a man was fishing from
the bridge, a duck family was paddling
downstream, and two boys were playing with
their boats. George would have liked to stop and look at
the boats, but he was afraid the boys might find out that
he had not delivered all the papers. So he rode on.

While riding along George kept thinking of boats all the time. It would be such fun to have a boat – but how could he get one? He thought and thought – and then he had an idea.

He got off the bicycle, took a newspaper out of the bag
and began to fold it.

First he folded down the corners, like this,

then he folded
both edges up,

brought the ends
together

and flattened it
sideways.

Then he turned
one corner up,

then the other one,

again brought the
ends together

and flattened it
sideways.

Then, gently, he pulled
the ends open –

and there was his BOAT!

Now the moment had come to launch the boat.

Would it float? It did!

So George decided to make some more boats. Finally
he had used up all the papers and had made so many
boats that he could not count them – a whole fleet.

Watching his fleet

sailing down the river George

felt like an admiral. But watching his fleet

he forgot to watch where he was going ...

suddenly there was a terrible jolt: the bicycle had hit

a rock and George flew off the seat, head first.

Luckily George was not hurt, but the front wheel of the
bicycle was all out of shape and the tyre was punctured.

George tried to ride the bicycle,

but of course it wouldn't go.

So he started carrying it, but it soon got too heavy.

George did not know WHAT to do: his new bike was

spoiled, the newspapers were gone. He wished he
had listened to his friend and kept close to the house.
Now he just stood there and cried...

Suddenly his face brightened. Why – he had forgotten that
he could ride on one wheel! He tried it and it worked.
He had hardly started out again when he saw something

he had never seen before: rolling towards him came an

enormous truck with huge trailers behind it. Looking out

of the trailers were all sorts of animals. To George it

looked like a zoo on wheels. The truck stopped and two

men jumped out. "Well, well," said one of the men, "a little monkey who can ride a bike bronco fashion! We can use you in our animal show tonight.

I am the director of the show and this is Bob.

He can straighten your wheel and fix that flat in no time and then we'll take you along to the place where the show is going to be."

So the three of them got into the cab and drove off.

"Maybe you could play a fanfare while you ride your bike
in the show," the director said. "I have a bugle for you
right here, and later on you'll get a green coat and a cap
just like Bob's."

On the show grounds everybody was busy getting things ready for the show. "I must do some work now," said the director. "Meanwhile you may have a look around and get

acquainted with all the animals – but you must not feed

them, especially the ostrich because he will eat anything

and might get very sick afterwards."

George was curious: would the ostrich really eat
anything. He wouldn't eat a bugle – or would he? George
went a little closer to the cage – and before he knew it

the ostrich had snatched the bugle and tried to swallow it.

But a bugle is hard to swallow, even for an ostrich;

it got stuck in his throat.

Funny sounds came out

of the bugle as the ostrich

was struggling with it,

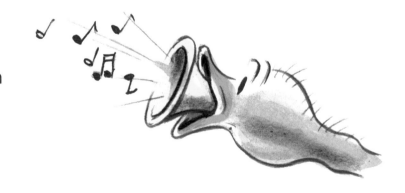

all blue in the face.

George was frightened.

Fortunately the men had heard a noise. They came rushing to the cage and got the bugle out of the ostrich's throat just in time.

The director was very angry with George. "We cannot use little monkeys who don't do as they are told," he said. "Of course you cannot take part in the show now. We will have to send you home."

George had to sit on a bench all by himself and nobody even looked at him. He was terribly sorry for what he had done but now it was too late. He had spoiled everything.

Meanwhile the ostrich, always hungry,

had got hold of a string dangling near his cage.

This happened to be the string

which held the door to the cage

of the baby bear. As the ostrich

nibbled at it the door opened –

and the baby bear got out.

He ran away as fast as he could and made straight for a high tree near the camp. Nobody had seen it but George – and George was not supposed to leave his bench. But this was an emergency, so he jumped up, grabbed the bugle, and blew as loud as he could. Then he rushed to his bicycle.

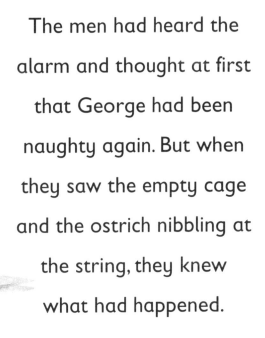

The men had heard the alarm and thought at first that George had been naughty again. But when they saw the empty cage and the ostrich nibbling at the string, they knew what had happened.

George raced towards the tree,

far ahead of the men.

By now the bear had climbed

quite high – and this was dangerous

because little bears can climb up

a tree easily but coming down

is much harder; they may

fall and get hurt.

The men were worried.

They did not know how

to get him down safely.

But George had his plan:

with the bag over his shoulder he went up the tree as fast

as only a monkey can, and when he reached the baby bear

he put him in
his bag and
carefully let him
down so that the
men could safely
catch him.

Everybody cheered when George had come down from the tree. "You are a brave little monkey," said the director. "You saved the baby bear's life. Now you'll get your coat back and of course you may ride your bike and play the bugle in the show."

Finally the show was on.
The whole town had come
to see it, and how surprised
they were to discover
George on his bike

right in the middle of it!
The newsboy was there
too and also the man
with the yellow hat

who had been looking for George everywhere and was happy to have found him at last. The newsboy was glad to have his bag again, and the people from the other side of the street whose papers George had made into boats were not angry with him any more.

George!

When the time had come for George to say goodbye, the
director let him keep the coat and the cap and the bugle.
And then George and his friend got into the car and went ...

good Night!